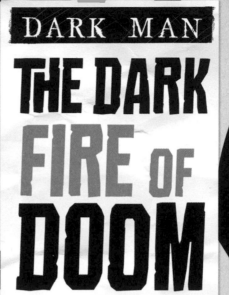

DARK MAN

THE DARK FIRE OF DOOM

BY PETER LANCETT

ILLUSTRATED BY JAN PEDROIETTA

Librarian Reviewer
Laurie K. Holland
Media Specialist (National Board Certified), Edina, MN
MA in Elementary Education, Minnesota State University, Mankato

Reading Consultant
Elizabeth Stedem
Educator/Consultant, Colorado Springs, CO
MA in Elementary Education, University of Denver, CO

STONE ARCH BOOKS
Minneapolis   San Diego

by Stone Arch Books
151 Good Counsel Drive, P.O. Box 669
Mankato, Minnesota 56002
www.stonearchbooks.com

Library of Congress Cataloging-in-Publication Data
Lancett, Peter.
    The Dark Fire of Doom / by Peter Lancett; illustrated by Jan
Pedroietta.
    p. cm. — (Zone Books. Dark Man)
    Summary: Old Man sends Dark Man into the tunnels to find and
extinguish a magic flame, the Fire of Doom, an evil gateway for demons.
    ISBN-13: 978-1-59889-864-4 (library binding)
    ISBN-10: 1-59889-864-7 (library binding)
    ISBN-13: 978-1-59889-924-5 (paperback)
    ISBN-10: 1-59889-924-4 (paperback)
    [1. Good and evil—Fiction. 2. Tunnels—Fiction.] I. Pedroietta,
Jan, ill. II. Title.
PZ7.L2313Daf 2008
[Fic]—dc22   2007003961

Art Director: Heather Kindseth
Graphic Designer: Kay Fraser

Photo Credits:
Digital Stock, cover; Rubberball Visuality, 4, 12, 14, 33

1 2 3 4 5 6 12 11 10 09 08 07

Printed in the United States of America

TABLE OF CONTENTS

In the dark and distant future, the Shadow Masters control the night. These evil powers threaten to cover the earth in complete darkness. One man has the power to stop them. He is the Dark Man — the world's only light of hope.

CHAPTER ONE

THE TUNNELS

Secret tunnels run under the **bad part** of the city.

 All the tunnels have an **awful smell.**

The Dark Man has been in the tunnels many times.

The Dark Man does not care how bad the tunnels smell.

The Dark Man can **hardly see** in the tunnel.

There is no 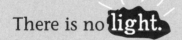light.

He steps very carefully.

The Dark Man looks for a
magic flame.

The Old Man said the **magic flame** was down here.

❨ CHAPTER TWO ❩

THE BOY

The Dark Man hears a **secret word** and stops.

A <u>boy</u> stands in front of him.

"I can take you to the **fire**," the boy says.

The Dark Man follows the **boy**.

The Dark Man **cannot see**
where they are going.

After a long walk, the boy **stops**.

"It is around the corner," he says.

19

« CHAPTER THREE »

THE FIRE

The Dark Man steps into the new tunnel alone.

A **flame burns** in the side of the wall.

This fire is a gateway used by **evil powers**.

The Dark Man knows what he must do.

He puts his **hand** into the flame.

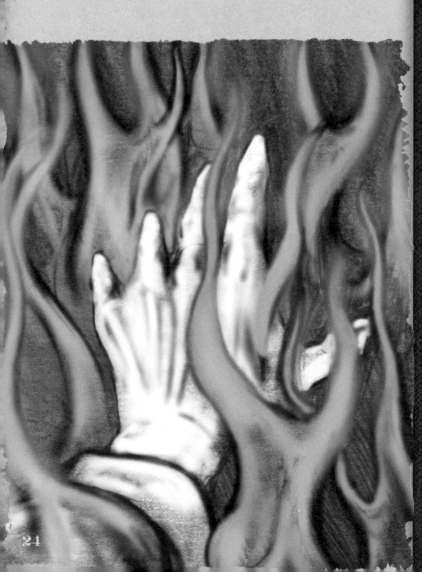

He has no **fear** so the fire does **not burn** him.

There is a great **flash**.

❰ CHAPTER FOUR ❱

IT IS DONE

When the Dark Man opens his **eyes**, he is lying on cool grass.

His hand is **not burned**.

He knows that the Fire of Doom will be **gone**.

He has  closed the gateway.

But there will be others.

The Dark Man can **never rest**.

The end . . . for now.

33

MORE LIGHT ON FIRE

In the story, fire is a powerful gateway for the Shadow Masters. Here are some facts about the power of fire in our own world:

Scientists have discovered evidence that early humans controlled fire 500,000 to 1.5 million years ago.

Fire gave early humans the power to scare away dangerous animals, move to colder areas of the world, and improve their diet.

Ancient civilizations created their own myths about how humans gained fire. For example, ancient Greeks believed the hero Prometheus (pruh-MEE-thee-us) stole fire from Mount Olympus, the home of their gods.

Humans are the only species with the power to control fire. Other species need it to live, such as the jewel beetle. This bug lays its eggs in the wood of burned trees.

Wildfires are powerful forces, but many of them can be prevented. In fact, humans start about 90% of wildfires with careless habits or even on purpose.

In 2000, wildfires destroyed a record 8.4 million acres of forests in the United States.

Wildfires can reach speeds up to 15 miles per hour. That's faster than you can run to escape it!

ABOUT THE AUTHOR

Peter Lancett was born in the city of Stoke-on-Trent, England. At age 20, he moved to London. While there, he worked for a film studio and became a partner in a company producing music videos. He later moved to Auckland, New Zealand, where he wrote his first novel, *The Iron Maiden*. Today, Lancett is back in England and continues to write his ghoulish stories.

ABOUT THE ILLUSTRATOR

Jan Pedroietta lives and works in Germany. As a boy, Pedroietta always enjoyed drawing and creating things from observing the world around him. He'd also spend many hours reading his brother's comic books about cowboys and American Indians. Today, comic books still inspire Pedroietta as he continues improving his own skills.

GLOSSARY

burned (BURND)—to be injured by fire

Fire of Doom (FY-ur UHV DOOM)—a flame through which evil powers and beings can enter the world

gateway (GAYT-way)—an opening, sometimes in a gate, through which things can pass

hope (HOHP)—to expect or wish something would happen

magic (MA-jik)—charms or spells that some people believe can make impossible things come true

power (POU-ur)—great strength and energy, or the ability to do something

DISCUSSION QUESTIONS

1. In the story, the Dark Man looks for the magic flame. Does he find it all by himself? Who helps him?

2. At the end of the story, the Dark Man knows that there will be other gateways. Do you think he will try to close them? Why or why not?

3. The author doesn't say where the little boy comes from. Do you think this secret makes the story more mysterious? Explain your answer.

WRITING PROMPTS

1. The Dark Man must explore some pretty scary places, but he can't be afraid. Describe something that frightens you. Write about how you deal with the fear.

2. The Dark Man never rests because there will be other gateways. Write your own story about how the Dark Man will find and close the next evil gateway.

3. This story feels somewhat like a dream, or maybe a nightmare. Write about the best or scariest dream you've ever had.

INTERNET SITES

Do you want to know more about subjects related to this book? Or are you interested in learning about other topics? Then check out FactHound, a fun, easy way to find Internet sites.

Our investigative staff has already sniffed out great sites for you!

Here's how to use FactHound:

1. Visit *www.facthound.com*

2. Select your grade level.

3. To learn more about subjects related to this book, type in the book's ISBN number: **1598898647**.

4. Click the **Fetch It** button.

FactHound will fetch the best Internet sites for you!